A Narrow Escape

and Other Stories

By Muriel Taylor

Edited by N. A. Woychuk

Copyright 1974 by N.A. Woychuk. All rights reserved. Printing or distribution of this book without written permission by the copyright owner is prohibited.

Scripture Memory Fellowship International

P. O. Box 411551 • St. Louis, Missouri 63141

ISBN 1-880960-08-7

Contents

	Page
A Narrow Escape	4
How Little Rattlesnake Got the Red Mark	8
Fireworks or Faith	11
The Boy Who Forgot	15
Bibles that Live	19
The Tidy Contest	25
The Three-Handed Girl	29
Putting Out the Lights	34
Miracle of Milk	37
On the Victory Side	42
A Dunce Who Became a Scholar	46
The Two Roses	49
The Cow Man's Quarter	54
A Cup of Cold Water	56
The Hurry-Hurry Song	59

Preface

In editing these excellent stories for publication, I have re-lived again the rich spiritual blessing I first gained from them as a boy while listening to Miss Muriel Taylor tell them to us at camp so effectively in her own special way. I am sure that her ministry contributed much to my salvation and my early Christian training.

Miss Taylor was the first secretary of the Canadian Sunday School Mission, with headquarters in Winnipeg, Manitoba. She served in this capacity most diligently for many years. She arranged various materials for camp and prepared the rich and instructive correspondence Bible courses which, I believe, the Mission is still using. Her life and work were indeed highly productive, and she "being dead, yet speaketh."

Many of these stories are based on actual experiences in the lives of people, both great and small. Each story expounds a certain Bible truth in a vivid and practical way.

We are delighted to be able to publish them. We believe that they will be read over and over again and will prove to be a real blessing not only in the lives of children and young people but also in the lives of adults.

We earnestly commend these choice story-illustrations to God and pray that He will be pleased to use them and multiply the blessing of Miss Taylor's ministry in days gone by in the lives of many thousands both now and in the years to come.

N. A. Woychuk
St. Louis, Missouri
October 19, 1973

A Narrow Escape

The boys at the Scout camp lounged around the bonfire. It had been a full day, and even the most energetic did not seem inclined for anything boisterous.

"Tell us some of your war experiences, Sir," one of the boys suggested to the Scoutmaster. The scouts considered him "pious, but tops." They respected him for his capability as a Scoutmaster, for his war record, and for the fact that though he "preached," he backed it up by his life.

"My war record was not unusual in any sense," the Scoutmaster replied.

"No narrow escapes?" questioned Jerry.

"One can hardly be in the war zone without some of those, but instead of my own narrow escapes, suppose I relate to you a true story of one of my friends. He hailed from Texas and was copilot of a Flying Fortress. One day while in the air, an oxygen box exploded, setting the large craft on fire and tearing a hole in it. One by one, the members of the crew used their parachutes, jumping clear of the burning plane. Before the last man went out, there came a second explosion which blew away my friend's parachute. The last man offered to share his parachute, but the offer was refused, for the two of them could never have squeezed through the escape hatch together. Here was my friend left alone and in danger of being roasted alive."

The Scoutmaster paused. The boys, hanging breathlessly on his words, cried, "Go on; go on. How did he get out?"

"By a miracle. He himself says it was a miracle in answer to his prayers, for he prayed plenty. I did not tell you that the plane was carrying a load of bombs. The fire was burning fast, and when it reached the bombs, you know what would happen. That might happen any moment."

Not a boy moved. There was no sound but the crackling of the fire. The Scoutmaster continued:

"Instruments were blacked out, but through a side window he could see he was over land, and he decided to try to bring the plane down onto the beach below. This landing required great skill, but he made it. He himself insists that of himself he never could have made the landing. But there was Someone else in control. When the plane was down, a new danger threatened. The section of the coast where the plane landed was heavily mined. Here was a further difficulty, but again there was provision for it. Coastguards were nearby who knew the path through the mines. So, leaving the burning plane and led by these men, he reached safety. Then, and only then, the plane with 2,000 pounds of bombs blew up."

The boys relaxed, and a sigh of relief went around the

circle. "What a thrill; wish I could have something like that happen to me. Tell us more," said Joe.

"About another narrow escape," Bob added.

"You have asked for it, fellows. Now you listen to this narrow escape as closely as you did to the other."

The man reached into his pocket and drew out a New Testament. Quickly he turned over the pages, 'til he found the place and read:

> "And one of the malefactors which were hanged railed on him, saying, If thou be the Christ, save thyself and us. But the other answering rebuked him, saying, Dost not thou fear God, seeing thou art in the same condemnation? And we indeed justly; for we receive the due reward of our deeds: but this man hath done nothing amiss. And he said unto Jesus, Lord, remember me when thou comest into thy kingdom. And Jesus said unto him, Verily I say unto thee, To day shalt thou be with me in paradise."

The strong quiet voice ceased.

"Don't see the narrow escape," remarked Bert; "he was crucified, wasn't he?"

"He escaped the outer darkness and the eternal separation from God that would have been his in a few hours if he had not acknowledged his sin. He turned to the Lord with a plea for mercy which was not refused. The way of escape today is just as simple as that."

The Scoutmaster turned over the pages of his New Testament, then with his finger on a verse, he asked Joe to read it. By the light of the fire the boy read, "How shall we escape if we neglect so great salvation?" Then turning to Bert, the man asked him to read another Scripture. Following the pointing finger, Bert read, "And why stand we in jeopardy every hour?"

"'Jeopardy' means 'danger,'" explained the leader. "My friend stood in danger every moment he continued in the bomb-loaded plane. There was a chance of escape, and he took it. Our God offers you not a chance, but a sure escape if you confess yourselves as sinners and accept the salvation He offers. Why do you fellows stand in danger every hour, for what other escape is there if you neglect this so great salvation?"

With these solemn words in their ears the boys went to bed. But before they slept some had made the great decision to accept the salvation God offers through personal faith in the Lord Jesus Christ.

Have you?

How Little Rattlesnake Got the Red Mark

Little Rattlesnake wasn't a rattlesnake, and he wasn't little. He was a full-grown man. How he came by such a name is not known, but maybe he had an adventure with a rattlesnake when he was a boy. You may not think it a nice name, but it was perfectly satisfactory to Little Rattlesnake and his friends, for he was a Hopi Indian living in Arizona.

As a boy, Little Rattlesnake learned to read and write at the government school. There was also a church on the reservation which he attended for a time, but he went back to the pagan practices of the Indians.

One night Little Rattlesnake went to bed to sleep and to dream. In his dream—a dream which was to change his life for time and eternity—he thought he was in his small house on the top of the hill. From there he could look down on the Indian village as he often did when awake. There was excitement among the Indians. When he looked for the cause, what he saw surprised him. A Person unknown to him was passing from house to house in the village, putting a red mark on some people and passing by others.

He put the mark on the missionary and his wife, as well as on others whom Little Rattlesnake knew as followers of "the Jesus Way."

Little Rattlesnake knew all about red marks, for like all Hopi Indians who are sheep owners, he marked his sheep with red paint. When telling his dream to someone later on he was asked, "What kind of a mark was it the Stranger put on the people?"

He replied, "A mark like Indians put on their sheep."

As this young man, in his dream, watched the mark being put on one and another, he hoped it might be placed on him, too. But the Stranger passed over his house and was gone. Then there came a great shout from above, and those who had the red mark on them began to go up in the air. As Little Rattlesnake followed them up, up, with his eyes, he saw they gathered in the upper air around a Person Whose face was brighter than the sun. Little Rattlesnake realized he had been left behind, and he was so frightened that he woke up.

"Oh, it's only a dream," and he turned over and went to sleep again, only to have the same dream again. When he awoke he said to his wife, "It's the Christians' God telling me they are right." He slept, and again the same dream came to him.

For days he was in distress. "Oh, I wish I had the red mark on me," was his cry, but he did not know how to get it. So great was his terror that when he heard there was to be a Christian Bible Conference in Flagstaff, he decided to attend and see if he could get help. As he entered the pavilion at Flagstaff where the meetings were held, a well-known minister, Dr. H. A. Ironside, was preaching. Now, prepare to be surprised! What do you think he was talking about as Little Rattlesnake came in? It was about the red mark! Our wonderful Lord so arranged matters that that day Dr. Ironside was preaching on the Passover, how God told the Israelites to put a red mark from the blood of a lamb on their doors, and how He said, "When I see the blood, I will pass over you."

"Ah, that's the red mark I'm looking for!" said Little Rattlesnake to himself. After the meeting, he spoke to the minister, who told the Indian of the blood that was shed by the Lord Jesus for our sins. He quoted many Bible verses such as, "Forasmuch as ye know that ye were not redeemed with corruptible things, as silver and gold, . . . but with the precious blood of Christ, as of a lamb without blemish and without spot."

For about fifteen minutes the Indian listened to the Scripture and the explanations without saying a word. Then he exclaimed joyfully, "I see it now. I've got the red mark."

There was a wonderful change in his life as all the Hopi Indians soon saw. Later he went to Bible School in Los Angeles to learn more about the Word of God. Then he went back to the reservation to spend the rest of his life telling his Indian friends how they could become one of the sheep in the fold of the Good Shepherd, how the Lord knows His own sheep by the blood mark on them (a mark He alone can see), and how when the Lord comes from heaven with a shout and the voice of the archangel, those who have the mark on them will be caught up to meet the Lord in the air, and so to be forever with the Lord.

No one is safe for eternity unless he has the red mark on him. We become one of His sheep, and He marks us, when we come to Christ as a sinner and accept His salvation.

Fireworks or Faith

On July 4th in the United States and May 24th in Canada, there are big displays of fireworks. They flash and make a show for a few seconds, then die out, and there is nothing left but burnt sticks and empty casings. Even the biggest and brightest last but a second or two. Fireworks are not lasting; they endure and amuse but for a season. How like the fleeting pleasures of the world. Yet some spend their lives seeking such things.

Selina may never have seen fireworks, for she was born in 1707. But even as a child, she wanted something more enduring than the empty joys the world can give. No doubt, people said of her, "What a lucky girl. She has beauty and title and wealth." Selina knew these things do not satisfy. Those outside her family called her the Lady Selina, for she was the daughter of an Earl.

One day little Selina and her sisters were walking with their nurse over the country hills, when they met a sad little procession. A handful of people followed a small coffin resting on the shoulders of four men. Selina was deeply moved. She had never been conscious of death before; now it was impressed upon her that life does not last. She asked questions. Who lay in the coffin? A little girl. How old? Nine years. A gloom settled over the child. Selina was nine years old!

At her desire, the nurse and the children followed the funeral to the cemetery. Selina noted where the grave was situated, under an old tree. Many a time in the years that followed, she would slip away from home to sit beside that grave, wondering about the little girl who would have been her age had she lived. Wonder where the child was. Wonder how she, Selina, could find something that would last, since life would end sooner or later.

So the years passed. Selina grew into a lovely young girl, admired and sought after, yet not happy. One night in the midst of a gay party, she felt she could no longer endure the bright lights and the compliments paid her. Afresh it came to her that pleasure is not lasting. Like a skyrocket, it blazes brilliantly for a moment, then dies out, leaving nothing but blackness. Without making any explanation, she had her carriage called and drove home from the party. In her room alone, she threw herself on her bed and wept bitterly. Where, oh where, could she find anything that was enduring?

She got the answer two years later. By then she had married and was the Countess of Huntingdon, her husband being a member of one of the noblest families in England. The answer to her question came through three things.

First: A testimony. Her husband's sister told her that she had trusted the Lord Jesus for salvation, and she said, "I'm as happy as an angel." The girl's face shone, and

Selina, Countess of Huntingdon, knew that she had found that which satisfies and lasts.

Second: A Book, or, shall I say, *The Book.* Recovering from a severe illness, the Countess began to read the Bible. She started with 1 Corinthians. In the first chapter and twenty-sixth verse, she found the words, " . . . not many wise . . . not many mighty, not many noble, are called." Afterwards she often said she was thankful for the letter "M" because if it had not been for that letter the verse would read, " . . . not any wise . . . not any mighty, not any noble, are called." The Countess read on until she came to the third chapter, verse eleven, "For other foundation can no man lay than that is laid, which is Jesus Christ." She began to see that though life, pleasure and wealth do not last, there is something sure and enduring.

Third: A preacher. Everybody in England had heard about a strange man named John Wesley, who was preaching in the fields and by the roadsides instead of in churches. Instead of reading his sermons like the ministers of that day, he spoke without a book before him. Selina had heard of him, but she had never heard him. So she went to hear Wesley preach. She never knew God could be so real to a person as He was to that man, who spoke with tears in his eyes about eternal things as if they really mattered.

Selina, Countess of Huntingdon, lifted up her heart to God, told Him she was but a poor sinner, and she trusted His mercy and grace for salvation. Scales seemed to fall from her eyes. She knew she had found what she sought. Indeed, she had, for the Gospel is no fireworks.

From that moment to the end of her life, she gave almost every penny of her wealth to spread the Gospel. She invited John Wesley to preach in the great drawing room of

Huntingdon Castle and asked the greatest people in the land to come and hear him. She explained the way of salvation to the poorest and humblest, as well as to princes, dukes and statesmen. She built churches everywhere, and when she had no more money, she sold all her jewels and built more. She sent missionaries to Africa, the South Seas and to the Indians.

For sixty years she found her happiness in this. At the age of eighty-four she lay on her death bed. Did she find that Jesus Christ is sufficient even in death? Her dying words were, "There is but one foundation on which a sinner like me can rest." As a little girl she longed for that which would be lasting and sure; as a young girl she cried for it; as a young woman she found the Lord Jesus, the sure foundation; and after sixty years she knew He was sufficient for death.

What about you? Are you going to build your life on those passing things that may be likened to fireworks? Or, through faith in Christ, on the one foundation that endures and satisfies through life and beyond?

The Boy Who Forgot

I wonder if in your house something like this takes place:

"John, did you remember to fill the wood box?"

"Oh, Mother, I forgot."

"Mary, did you remember to give my message to the teacher?"

"Oh, I forgot all about it."

Most of us have good "forgetteries."

In that wonderful book, *Pilgrim's Progress*, the boys, Matthew and Samuel, travel with Mr. Great-heart, and they come to a place which is called "Forgetful Green." And Mr. Great-heart tells the boys that "Forgetful Green" is a most dangerous place to stay in. So if any of you are living in "Forgetful Green," you had better move out quickly.

Many years ago there lived a boy who had a bad memory. Now there's nothing worth making a story about in that, for almost every boy has a bad memory. But this boy learned something he never forgot, and that's what makes his story worthwhile.

John was this boy's name, and he lived more than 200 years ago. When he was only a baby, his mother knelt beside his bed many times, committing him to God, and asking God to make her baby a lover of Him. And as he got older, John would kneel beside her and pray with her. But when he was only seven, his mother left him for her heavenly home.

And then John forgot. He forgot his mother's prayers, the Scripture verses she had taught him, forgot how his mother wanted him to be a Christian. Four years after her death, he went to sea, a little fellow only eleven years of age. Among rough and godless companions, the memory of his mother's prayers faded.

Sometimes he would remember. Once while yet a boy, he was thrown from a horse and almost killed. Back came the memory of the God his mother loved and Whom he had neglected. But in writing of it after, he said, "I soon forgot."

Another time he and some companions were going out in a boat. John was detained, and his friends did not wait. The boat upset and everyone was drowned. John went to the funeral. He was deeply impressed as he thought but that for the fact he was detained, he, too, would be lying cold in death. After the funeral it left his mind, and again he *forgot.*

Meanwhile, he was visiting all sorts of strange places as a sailor. He went to Africa and became a slave trader; and then, going from bad to worse, he became a slave himself, his owner a Negro woman who treated him very cruelly.

Escaping from that life, he went to sea again. On shipboard he had a remarkable dream. The ship was on its way home from Italy, and John lay in his hammock. He dreamed and knew he was on the ship. It was midnight, the time of his watch on deck. A Stranger came to him and gave him a lovely ring set with sparkling jewels. He thanked the Stranger with the beautiful face and shining eyes and gracious manner. "Don't lose it, or you will have nothing but misery," said the Stranger, and vanished.

Then another stranger appeared, but so different from the first one. A scowling face, a hard mouth, and a cruel expression was his. Pointing to the ring, "Throw it away," he commanded in a harsh voice.

John listened to the voice of this second stranger. Going to the side of the ship he threw the gleaming ring far into the sea where it sank beneath the waves. Suddenly the water was ablaze with fire, and in his dream John knew that the ring was his soul given to him by none other than the Lord Jesus, the gracious Stranger. He had thrown it away at the direction of Satan, the second stranger. The fire stood for judgment, and his soul was being destroyed in it.

In great sorrow, John watched the place where his ring had disappeared. Suddenly the first Stranger was by his side. "O, get it back for me, the ring which is my soul," John cried.

The Stranger plunged into the burning water; for a time, He was lost to view, and John thought He had perished. Then He reappeared with the ring in His hand. "Give it to me, O, give it to me," implored John, falling at His feet. But the Stranger said, "No, you let Me keep it for you, and it will never be lost."

John awoke and knew that this dream had been sent to him by God; it was another plea to him to let Christ save him and keep him. He thought about the dream for a long time, and then he *forgot* it.

Came a day he was never to forget—March 10, 1748. The ship he was on was caught in a terrible storm. Plunging up and down in the trough of the waves, none of the sailors ever expected to reach land again. The hold of the ship was filling with water.

"To the pumps," commanded the captain. As John went to take his place at the pumps, he said to the captain, "May the Lord have mercy on us." As he worked the pumps he thought of his own words. "Mercy, mercy, can there be mercy for me who has forgotten God all these years?"

At six o'clock that evening, the hold was free from water, and hope began to spring up in hearts that they might yet live. John stopped pumping and began to pray—pray for mercy. And he found it on March 10, 1748.

He never was troubled with failing memory again. Always he took special note of March 10th as it came round year by year. He became a Christian minister, and then he printed with his own hand a text from the Bible and hung it in his study where he could always see it. The text was this: "And thou shalt remember that thou wast a bondman . . . and the Lord thy God redeemed thee."

John's full name was John Newton, and he wrote many of the hymns we sing: "How Sweet the Name of Jesus Sounds," "One There is Above All Others," "O How He Loves," and many others, When he was an old man at the end of life's pilgrimage, he made this statement, "My memory is nearly gone, but I remember two things. I am a great sinner, and Christ is a great Savior." If you remember these two things, boys and girls, your memory will be a blessing to you.

Bibles that Live

"Likewise, ye wives, be in subjection to your own husbands; that, if any obey not the word, they also may without the word be won by the conversation of the wives; while they behold your chaste conversation . . . whose adorning let it not be that outward adorning of plaiting the hair, and of wearing of gold, or of putting on of apparel; but let it be the hidden man of the heart, . . . even the ornament of a meek and quiet spirit, which is in the sight of God of great price" (1 Peter 3:1-4).

These verses are addressed to "wives," but they are not limited to them. This passage tells us that there are people who will not read the Word of God, but they do read the lives of Christians and may be won to Christ if our lives are right. The poet has said something the same:

"You are the only Bible the careless world will read;

You are the sinners' Gospel; you are the scoffers' creed."

Shall we take the letters of the word "Bible" and consider what kind of a Bible that lives will win others to Christ?

19

B-eginning—

The written Bible begins with the words, "In the beginning God." There must be a time when you begin to be a Bible that lives, and you cannot do it without God. Christ must be accepted as your Savior, and then quiet time must be spent with God over His Book and in prayer. The younger you begin, the better.

Over one hundred years ago a man called Tischendorff visited a monastery at Mount Sinai. In a wastepaper basket he discovered some pages of Greek writing. He looked at it closely and saw that it was a very old version of the New Testament. But the beginning was missing. He asked the monks about it, and they told him that they used the first pages to light the fire. It is the oldest manuscript we have, but the beginning is lost because the monks burned it up. It is a very valuable manuscript, but not so valuable as it would have been had the beginning not been lost.

I wonder if some of you are like this manuscript, wasting the years of your youth apart from God. Remember, you can never get a lost beginning back. It is gone forever. There is no better time than when you are young to begin to be a Bible that lives.

I-nside—

Among the Africans to whom Robert Moffatt taught the Word of God was an old African Chief who had a very keen hunting dog. One day he came to Mr. Moffatt in great distress. "My dog has eaten your New Testament," said he.

"That is too bad," replied the missionary, "but I don't think it will harm your dog, for he is able to eat big bones, and a little book will not make him sick."

"O, it's not that," said the Chief. "But your Book is so

full of love and gentleness, I'm afraid my dog will never be good for hunting again."

Look at the text at the beginning of this story. It tells us what the "Bibles that live" should be like on the inside. The spirit should be meek and quiet. Meek means the opposite of quarrelsome. Few of us are meek by nature. Moses was not, but he became the meekest man on earth (Numbers 12:3). That was because he spent much time alone with God. Once it was forty days and nights with Him, and his proud spirit, his quarrelsome nature, became peaceable and gentle. Christ is meek and lowly in heart, and He bids us learn of Him. Remember, you won't get a humble, gentle spirit just by hoping or resolving. "Learn of me; for I am meek and lowly in heart." We learn of Him through His Word and prayer.

B-inding—

The cover or dress of the Bible is usually black, but not necessarily so. I have seen red Bibles, bright blue Bibles and lovely white ones. The binding is not important, but it is the first thing people notice about a Bible.

And it may be the first thing unbelievers notice about a Christian. There are two mistakes young people are liable to make in regard to their dress, girls especially. If the appearance is untidy, hands soiled, clothing out-of-date, non-Christians think that it is Christianity that makes one careless and indifferent to outward appearances. On the other hand, in His Word quoted at the beginning, God tells us we are not to think too much of our clothes, of our "outward adorning." Too much time and money spent on this is not becoming to a Christian. So do not make the mistake of thinking too little about your appearance (boys often fail here), nor too much about it (this is often the girls' weakness).

How, then, as Christians, shall we strike a happy medium between these two extremes? If we love the Lord with all our heart, the question will settle itself. We will see that God has first claim on our time, our money and our affections, and our dress will fall into second place. Neither will we want to dishonor Him by a careless appearance that may lead unbelievers to misjudge Christianity.

A story may help here. On September 3, 1939, the passenger ship, "Athenia," was sunk by the enemy. Men, women and children perished. But some were saved, among them a young woman who was coming to Canada to be married. She brought off the sinking ship a small suitcase which she never let out of her hands. When the passengers in the life boat were taken on board the rescue ship, "City of Flint," she carried the suitcase; when they landed at Halifax, she was still guarding it. She told friends it contained her wedding gown. The long journey by train started, the case still in her hands. At Winnipeg she was met by her bridegroom. Then for the first time she dropped the suitcase and ran to meet him. The precious dress meant much to her until she had him. Then it took second place.

L-abel—

Your mother, when she makes jam, puts a label on the jar to tell what is within. There is a label on the Word of God. Look at your copy, and you will see the label reads "Holy Bible." That tells what the contents of the Book are. People wear labels that tell what is within, and the owner cannot prevent others from reading it. Your face is your label. What you are is written on your face. Anger, fear, pride, selfishness, hate, all leave their mark on the face. So does contentment, love and peace. A true Christian usually can be recognized by the face.

In the Boxer Rebellion in China when wicked men were killing all Christians, they knew Chinese Christians by their faces.

Many years ago in a town in the United States, the missionary, Adoniram Judson, was expected to speak at one of the churches. He arrived by an earlier train than planned, and, of course, no one was there to meet him. But there was a small boy at the station who ran home and told his father that the missionary had come.

"How do you know, for you have never seen Mr. Judson?"

"Oh, but I know he is the missionary because of his face," was the boy's reply.

Years after, when he was Editor of the *Sunday School Times,* he wrote a booklet entitled, "What a Boy Saw in a Missionary's Face."

Remember Stephen, who had "the face of an angel" in the midst of the wicked men plotting to kill him. Remember Moses, whose face shone when he came down from the mountain where he had been talking with God. Their faces gave them away.

What kind of a label are you carrying around with you? The outside shows what is inside.

E-nding—

The Bible has an ending, and yet, it has not an ending. As far as its written words are concerned it ends. But its influence will never end. So it is with those who live for God.

Look at these ten names and see if you can remember anything about the ten men who bore the names:

Shammua	Gaddiel	Sethur
Shaphat	Gaddi	Nahbi
Igal	Geuel	
Palti	Ammiel	

I have asked even ministers, and they have said they never heard of these ten men. Yet they are in the Bible (Numbers 13).

Now here are two more names:

    Caleb   Joshua

Of course, you know about these two. The first ten were the spies who brought back an evil report of the promised land, because they looked at the giants instead of God. The last two had no fear of the giants, because their trust was in God. The first ten have been forgotten; the influence of the last two is still going on.

B-eginning, I-nside, B-inding, L-abel, and E-nding go to make up the written Bible and the Bible that lives.

"You are writing a Gospel, a chapter each day,
  By the things that you do and the words that you say.
  Men read what you write, whether faithless or true,
  Say, what is the Gospel according to YOU?"

The Tidy Contest

Aunt Pollie was distressed, but, being a wise person, she did not say anything to her nieces and nephew immediately. "I will wait until they know me and love me before I speak about it," she thought.

What was it she was to speak about? If you saw the untidy bedrooms of the three young Nortons, if you had followed them around for one day picking up the articles they dropped just anywhere when through with them, you would know why Aunt Pollie was distressed. Perhaps it was not altogether the children's fault, for their mother died some years before, and one housekeeper after another had been in charge. Now Aunt Pollie had come, a great improvement on housekeepers, the three children agreed.

A few weeks later, Aunt Pollie had a serious talk with the children one morning about the matter of their untidiness. Then, "How would you like to have a contest? Each one write out the best reasons for being orderly and neat. Tonight we will read what you have thought up, and—two helpings of dessert to the one who suggests the best reasons."

The contest was on. Pauline's pencil scribbled busily and seemed to be doing more scratching out than writing. Madeline spent several hours in the library consulting books. No one knew what Hugh was up to, for he shut himself in his bedroom for most of the day.

In the evening, the three gathered expectantly in the living room, with their Aunt as judge of the contest in the center of the little group.

"Ladies first, Hugh, so we'll begin with the girls. All right, Pauline."

Pauline's sheet of paper was no recommendation for neatness. No one but the writer could have made out the scrawl with the many erasures. But when read, it sounded as it might win the prize, at least to Pauline's ears.

"Reasons why we should be tidy:
1. Because it makes more work for other people if we are not.
2. Because it's easier to find things if we are.
3. Because the house looks better tidy, and so do we.

And I've written a poem as a horrible example to us Nortons. Just listen to it:

>   There's a family no one wants to meet,
>   They live, it is said, on Untidy Street,
>   In the city where nothing is ever in order,
>   And the river of Carelessness marks its border.
>   Their buttons are off, and their shoes don't shine,
>   I wouldn't want this family for mine.
>   So it would be wisest to keep your feet
>   From this city where no one ever is neat.
>   Always be tidy whatever you do,
>   Lest folks think this is your family, too."

Aunt Pollie commended the first contestant, after which Madeline took the floor. "I'm going to tell you how tidy ants are, a-n-t-s, not A-u-n-t-s."

"A-u-n-t-s are, too," laughed Pauline, "but let's hear about ants."

"Ants are interesting I found out, and very tidy. Harvesting ants plant grain and harvest it, too. They never allow a weed to grow in the ground they have planted. When husking the ripe seeds they don't litter up their nests with the trash, but throw the husks outside. The white ant is so carefully clean that it eats its garbage!"

"Don't try that on us, Aunt Pollie!" put in Hugh.

"The ants build their nests in a very orderly way, with neat passages. And they are so tidy about themselves. Do you know, ants have little combs and toothbrushes on their feet! When they have any time to spare, they spend it in polishing and dusting themselves. That's all about ants, but as for me, I'm not going to let a little ant beat me. From this time on I'll be as neat as an ant."

It was Hugh's turn. "I'll have to take you upstairs for my reason." So upstairs they all marched. The boy threw open the door of his room. O what a change! The books which usually were piled on chairs or the floor were neatly arranged in the bookcase. Hugh's clothes were hung on the hooks of the closet instead of thrown on the floor. On the floor of the closet, his shoes were standing side by side, "so they can chat with one another," as Hans Anderson says in one of his fairy tales.

"I'm going to keep it that way," Hugh said. "I want to please you, Aunt Pollie, because I love you. That's my reason."

Tears came to the Aunt's eyes, and she said nothing.

27

Neither did the girls for several seconds. Then Pauline spoke, "I think Hugh should get the second helping of dessert." And Madeline nodded agreement.

Boys and girls, the Lord Jesus says in His Book, "If ye love me, keep my commandments." That's the way we can show our love to Him. Do you know what His commandments are? You will find them in the Bible.

The Three-Handed Girl

Sally Brown was the nicest girl; everyone liked her. But she had one bad fault—she was seldom on time.

"Wash the dishes," her mother would say.

"Yes, Mother," Sally would reply, and she would stand with a cup in one hand and a spoon in the other, just playing with them and dreaming.

"Sally, have you swept the floor?"

"Not yet, Mother. There's lots of time," Sally would reply.

School days were worse.

"You'll be late for school," her brother Bob would say.

"Oh, there's lots of time. Anyway, you'll give me a ride, won't you, so that I'll get there by the time the bell rings." And Bob would give her a ride, so that she was not so often as late as she might have been.

It was the same when her Sunday school teacher talked to her about giving her heart to Christ. "There's lots of time; I'm only twelve." The next year she said, "Oh, I'm only thirteen—lots of time."

It got so bad, this habit of hers of always being late, that one day her mother said, "Sally, I don't know what we're going to do about you. You never do anything beforehand."

Her brother, Bob, on hearing this, called out, "Right hand! left hand! behind hand!—three-handed Sally." The name stuck, but even that didn't cure Sally of always being late.

Sally came home from school one day very excited. That year all the junior high schools were studying Tennyson's "Idylls of the King." The school where Sally attended had been invited to send the best students to recite portions of that poem in competition with the junior high school in the next town. The best reciters had been chosen, and everyone was looking forward to the trip. "And I'm to be one of them," Sally said, "not to recite, but there's a song in it, and I'm the best singer in the class."

When Sally showed the family what she had to sing, Father laughed, and Bob said, "It must have been written especially for three-handed Sally."

Even her mother said, "If it wasn't so solemn a subject, Sally, I'd be amused, too."

But Sally didn't care. She was too thrilled at the thought of the journey and the part she was to take. She practiced her song over and over.

"Do you know what it means?" Mother asked her.

Sally didn't.

"Tennyson based that song on the story of the ten virgins in the Bible. Five were wise, and five were foolish. The wise ones had their lamps all filled with oil, waiting for the Bridegroom to come; but the foolish had no oil. When the Bridegroom was announced, the foolish ones went off in a hurry to buy oil. While they were away, the Bridegroom came; the wise virgins went in with Him to the marriage supper, and the door was shut. Then the foolish virgins came knocking at the closed door, asking to be admitted, but it was too late. Now try your song again, remembering the story.

Sally did. She sang it solemnly and sweetly:

"'Late, late, so late, and dark the night and chill.
Late, late, so late, but we can enter still.
Too late, too late; ye cannot enter now.

'No light had we, for this we do repent.
And learning this the bridegroom will relent.
Too late, too late; ye cannot enter now.

'No light, so late, and dark and chill the night,
O let us in that we may find the light.
'Too late, too late; ye cannot enter now.'"

"It's a sad song," said Sally, "but I understand it better now that you have told me the story."

The day of the trip came at last. The train left in the morning at eleven o'clock. Sally had a new white dress to wear, and she spent a long time putting it on.

"Hurry," called her mother.

"Lots of time," said Sally.

The hands of the clock went on going round. Mother looked at it two or three times, but she didn't call again. At last Sally was ready. She came down and looked at the clock.

"Why—why, Mother, it's only ten minutes to train time. Why didn't you call me?"

"I did once, Sally, but it's time you learned a lesson. If you catch the street car, you'll just get to the station in time.

Sally dashed out of the house just in time to see the car

disappearing round the corner. No time to wait for another. She started running for the station as fast as she could. A long street led right through the town. At the end was the station. The tracks ran across the street, and when a train was ready to pass on the tracks, large iron gates closed across the street to keep cars and people from crossing in front of the train. Sally could see these gates, and as long as they were open she knew the train was still in the station. Faster and faster she ran. The nice ribbon that had taken her fifteen minutes to put in her hair fell off, but she did not stop to pick it up. Her breath was almost gone; her face was red from the heat and the exertion of running. But the gates were still open, so on she went, more and more quickly.

Would she ever get there? Only two more blocks, and the gates were still open! Only one block now, and the gates were not closed! She tried to run faster, but she couldn't. Only a step or two more. Quick! Quick! Just as she reached the iron gates—so close she could touch them, they slammed into place. The gates were shut.

Sally shook them as hard as she could. "Open them; open them!" she cried.

An old man with a long grey beard, who had just been going to cross when the gates closed, said, "It's no use, missy; when they're closed, they're closed."

"But I must get through!" cried Sally. "I must, I must! Why, they can't have the school concert without me."

Even as she spoke, the train thundered by on its way.

"Too bad," said the old man. "But it's too late now. I wonder, little miss," he went on, "if you have ever heard this verse from the Bible: 'Strive to enter in at the strait gate: for many, I say unto you, will seek to enter in, and shall not be able. When once the master of the house is risen up, and hath shut to the door, and ye begin to stand without, and to knock at the door, saying, Lord, Lord, open unto us; and He shall answer and say unto you, I know you not whence ye are.' Ah, little miss, that'll be a lot worse, to have that door shut against you than this one. Make sure of heaven before it is too late, by receiving Jesus Christ as your Savior."

Sally thought about his words as she walked home sadly. They fitted right into the song she would have sung. She remembered her Sunday school teacher's invitation to come to Christ, as well as her reply that there was lots of time. Was there? She had thought she had lots of time to catch the train, but she was too late. Might it be that she could put off salvation so long that she might hear the words, "Too late, too late, ye cannot enter now," and find the door of heaven shut?

This experience led Sally to accept Christ as her Savior, and she became an earnest Christian. And I'm glad to tell you that she also mended her ways about being behind time in other things until Bob had to give up calling her the three-handed girl.

Putting Out the Lights

"I don't want to go to church today," said Jack to his mother one fine Sunday morning.

"Do you feel sick, Jack?" she asked.

"No, I'm all right—and I'm not going to Sunday school either," he added defiantly.

"Why not?" his mother asked him quietly.

"Oh, I'm too big for Sunday school; it's all right for little ones, but I'm twelve, and past that. What's the use of church and Sunday school, anyhow? There's lots of other things to be doing on Sunday. I can be playing baseball, or I can go into town and have a good time with the other fellows."

His mother made no answer for a moment. Then she said, "I suppose next thing you'll be saying is, 'What's the use of the Bible? Better read some more exciting book.'"

"Well, why not?" This from Jack in a sulky tone, "I'm tired of hearing Bible stories."

Jack's mother talked no more with him, but perhaps she talked to God about him. I rather think she did. Any-

34

how, that night Jack had a dream. It was a strange dream. He thought he met a wretched looking old man, a horrid, snarly, unhappy old fellow. This old man greeted Jack as if he were a friend.

"Hello, Jack, don't you know me?"

"No, I don't," said Jack, and to himself he whispered, "I don't want to know you." Then aloud, "Who are you, anyhow?"

"I'll tell you. I'm YOU."

"Me!" Jack was indignant. "Indeed, you are not."

"Yes, I'm you—just what you'll be sixty years from now if you go on as you are now."

"I don't believe it," cried the little boy.

"I'll show you, then. You see that?" and the old man pointed down a long, dark tunnel. "That tunnel is life, and it's a pretty dark business for a boy like you to go through the tunnel without lights to guide."

"But there are lights! I can see them glowing right to the end."

"Yes," replied the old fellow, "but on your way to becoming what I am, you have already begun to put them out."

Jack was puzzled. Much as he hated to talk with such a disagreeable man, he continued with him to find out his meaning.

They entered the tunnel together. Just above them glowed a bright lamp marked "God's Word," which the old man suddenly turned out, leaving the tunnel darker than before.

"Oh, what have you done?" exclaimed Jack.

"Done?" mumbled the old fellow. "Why, I have only done what you have already done. You said you were tired of hearing the Word of God."

On they went to the next light, which was marked "Prayer." Up went the hand of the old man, and in a moment that light was out.

"It was your hand that did that, Jack," said his companion, and Jack remembered how lately he had never knelt down morning or evening to speak with God. He thought he was too old for that.

On they went until they reached another lamp marked "Sunday School," and in a moment, the light was turned out.

"No need of that light," growled the old fellow. "What's the use of it, anyhow?" And Jack remembered his words to his mother earlier in the day.

The next light was named "The Lord's Day."

"This is of no use," and the light was turned out.

Then on to the next—the one light left, "God's House."

"Now you see what you have done, Jack," snarled the old fellow. "You have put out all the lights! See how easy it is to put out this last one."

And in a flash the old fellow put it out.

"But what is left?" cried Jack in anguish.

"Nothing!" was the reply. "Nothing but the dark tunnel in which you walk without God and without hope until sixty years from now, when you'll be just like I am!"

"Oh, I don't want to put the lights out! I need them." And as he cried this in real distress, Jack awoke.

But he never again asked to stay home from church or Sunday school. He saw that if he was to grow up to be a happy man, a man whose life was worthwhile, a man whom people respected, he needed these lights. And they would help guide him home to the City of God, where there is no darkness at all.

Miracle of Milk

In a little home in the heart of Africa, a missionary mother was carefully counting the tins of milk on the shelf. She was getting ready to return to the United States for their rest period. The date to leave their station had been set, but at the last moment it had to be changed to two weeks later.

This was serious, because of the milk. There are no cows in that part of Africa, and the milk for this mother's baby and two other little children had to come in tins all the way from England. Knowing the date they were to leave, the mother had ordered just enough milk for the time they would be on the mission station. The tins of milk were getting to be very few, but with care the mother thought she could make them last for the extra two weeks.

Then Njambi came to the mission station with her baby in her arms to see if the missionary could help. What a pitiful little object that little baby was—only skin and bones, its little fingers like bird's claws, and its tiny wail (for it was too weak to cry loudly) went right home to the missionary's heart. There was a little grave on the hillside nearby where one of the missionary mother's own babies had been laid to rest, and her heart was tender toward all babies, especially sick ones. She knew what was the matter with Njambi's baby. She knew what would put flesh on its tiny bones and bring it back to life. It needed milk.

The native babies in that land are so poorly fed that many of them die in infancy. The heathen mothers in their ignorance stuff the babies with whatever food is cooked for the grownups—cornmeal mush, millet gruel, even mashed bananas. The babies have to be healthy to live through this. Only Christian mothers, trained in the mission schools, have learned how to feed their children properly.

Yes, Njambi's little one needed milk. But where was it to be gotten? The missionary mother looked at the cans of milk on her shelf. There were not many of them, for a sufficient number of cans for the journey had already been packed. It would take every can on the shelf to restore health to Njambi's baby, and what would happen to her own little ones without milk, especially the baby? Milk is even more important in French Equatorial Africa than here, because all food is short. Two voices began to talk within her.

The first voice said, "Your children will get ill if they don't have milk, and how can you start on a long journey with sick children?"

The second voice said, "But Njambi's baby will die if it does not have milk."

The first voice said, "Why should you take milk away from your little ones for her child?"

The second voice said, "Because you have come here to show the love of God to these people, and the only way they can know the love of God to them is to see you showing love to them."

The missionary lifted her voice in prayer that God would guide her. Then she knew. Going to the shelf, she took down the precious cans of milk, showed the African mother how to prepare the milk for her child, and sent her home with new hope.

The mother watched Njambi go down the hill from the mission station with the milk that might be carrying health away from her own children, and it seemed as if her faith and courage went with Njambi. There was only one thing for her to do, and she did it. She went down on her knees in prayer. She reminded the Lord that *her* baby was now without milk, and, unless He worked a miracle, the child would suffer. She told Him she had done what she felt was right, but her faith was weak and her heart fearful for her children. She asked Him to provide for them, comfort her own heart, and give her the assurance that the children would be taken care of.

Then she opened her Bible. Do you know that there is something in the Bible to fit every need? This mother proved this. She opened the Book with the prayer that God would give her something from it to bring hope to her heart. Without looking especially for any one place, she found staring her in the face a verse she never knew was in the Bible that exactly fitted her need. It was Proverbs 27:27: "And thou shalt have goats' milk enough for thy food, for the food of thy household, and for the maintenance for thy maidens."

Joyfully, she rose from her knees. God had answered

from His Word. It would be all right. When her husband came in, she told him how she had given away the children's milk and added, "But the Lord is going to provide goats' milk for the children."

"Well," was her husband's answer, "it will be a miracle, for there is only one flock of goats anywhere near here, and Aduba takes the full supply for himself and his family."

The missionary mother did not permit herself to be disturbed. She believed God had spoken, and He would perform.

It was not long 'til she saw someone coming up the hill. As he got closer, she recognized the merchant from the village, Aduba by name—the one to whom her husband had referred. He was not a Christian, had not even seemed to be interested in the Gospel. Here he was approaching the mission house. And his errand? It was soon stated, "I am leaving with my family for several weeks' visit, and I will have no need of the milk I get from the goats. I would be glad to have it delivered to you if you can use it."

Of course, you know what the reply was. God had given the goats' milk for her "household" and her "maidens," according to Proverbs 27:27. Thus, until the time they left, the children had all the milk they could drink.

To give up her children's milk meant more sacrifice on the part of that mother than most people living in Canada and the United States can realize.

The Bible is spoken of as milk in 1 Peter 2:2. I wonder if you boys and girls have ever sacrificed to give that Milk to the children in heathen lands, who are dying without it? Why not have a little collection box and give—not what you can spare, but what you can't spare. That's the way this missionary mother gave. That's the way God gave when He sent the Lord Jesus down to this earth. But remember, we must first give ourselves to the Lord Jesus, and then our prayers and our gifts for those in heathen lands.

On the Victory Side

Once upon a time there was a boy called Henri Duval living in the city of London, England. You may say, "Henri Duval—that does not sound like an English name," and you would be right. He had been brought to England from his native land of France while a small child, and he grew up among English companions and English surroundings. At times, he almost forgot he was French! That is, until one day when he realized that he was, indeed, French.

It was in school, and the history lesson that day covered the battle of Waterloo. Now for the first time Henri learned that in 1815, in the little village of Waterloo, the great French leader, Napoleon, with his armies, made his stand against the British forces led by the Duke of Wellington and was so totally defeated that it ended his career as a soldier. Since Henri was the only French boy in the class, he found the story rather embarrassing, especially since many of the boys turned and looked at him, as much as to say, "Well, we finished you off that time."

Henri went home troubled. "I don't like to be beaten," he told his father, to which the father replied, "The French were the losers in the battle of Waterloo. That's history, and you can't change history." Henri saw that was true, but it did not make the French overthrow any easier to take.

"I don't ever want to hear of Waterloo again," he declared. "I shall tear that page out of my history book! I like to be on the victory side always."

Some weeks went by, and one day his father called him to him. "Henri, I have something to tell you. Today is an important day. I have received my naturalization certificate making me a British subject."

Henri did not know what that meant, so his father explained that after a person has lived a certain time in a country which is not his own by birth, he can become a citizen of that country with the same rights and privileges as those born in that country.

"What did you have to do, Father, in order to become a British citizen?"

"I had to renounce my allegiance to France and promise loyalty to the British Crown."

"Did you have to do that in order to live in this land?"

"No, it is entirely my choice. But it seemed the best thing to do, since my business and home are here."

Henri wanted to know one more thing: "What difference will it make to us, Father?"

The father thought for a moment and then he said, "Well, there's one important difference that I think will appeal to you, Henri. Before I made this choice the battle of Waterloo was a defeat—now it's a victory. As I said, you can't change history, but you can change sides. Now we're on the victory side."

That conversation came back to Henri the following summer. He went with some of his chums to a Christian camp for boys. Around the bonfire one evening, the leader,

Mr. Gordon, gave them a Gospel talk on the text, "Choose ye this day whom ye will serve." During the address Henri's mind went back to the time when his father, although French by birth, became British by choice. He saw that by nature and birth, he belonged to the kingdom of sin and Satan, for Mr. Gordon read to them Ephesians 2:3, that we were " . . . by nature the children of wrath." But there was another kingdom, which the Bible calls, "the kingdom of God's dear Son."

It's the kingdom of Christ, Who defeated Satan by His death on the cross for the sins of the world and Who conquered death by rising from the grave. So it's a victorious kingdom.

How clearly Henri saw that just as his father had given up his allegiance to France and by his choice had become a British subject, so he, Henri Duval, could choose to change from the kingdom of darkness, where he was constantly being defeated by sin, to the kingdom of God. His father had made his choice nationally; now Henri made his spiritually and personally.

When opportunity was given for those who would do so to accept Christ, Henri rose, and in a clear, firm voice, said, "I choose Christ." That moment Henri passed from death to life, from the kingdom of darkness to the kingdom of God's dear Son, from the sin side to the victory side. Before leaving the bonfire, the boys sang a chorus, which was to become a great favorite with the French boy who liked to be on the victory side. They sang:

> "On the victory side, On the victory side,
> No fears can haunt me, no foe can daunt me,
> With Christ within, the fight we'll win,
> On the victory side."

Boys and girls, do not put off making your choice 'til you are old. None are too young to sin, none are too young to need the Savior from sin. Choose Christ if you have not done so, and move over to the victory side.

A Dunce
Who Became a Scholar

I wonder if you boys and girls ever count your buttons, saying that old rhyme, "Tinker, tailor, soldier, sailor," and so on through all the professions, good and bad? There is one vocation not mentioned there, and yet it is one of the most honorable—that of missionary. It is one of the happiest and most worthwhile callings there is. This is a story about a boy who became a missionary; and he came to that decision when he was not very old. Yet, there never seemed to be a more unlikely person to become a missionary than Robert, when he was young.

There was no doubt about it: the children at school first began to say it; the neighbors started to repeat it; even his parents began to think it; yes, Robert was a *dunce*, just too stupid to learn. The boy hated school, perhaps because the teacher was his uncle, and he was stern and strict with his nephew. School in those days was not as pleasant as you find it today, for this happened nearly 200 years ago.

If Robert did not learn at school, he learned at home.

His home was a poor one, but rich in other things than money. Every morning his father took down the big Bible and read it and prayed with his family. His mother loved the Scriptures, too, and knew what a blessing it is to memorize the Word of God. (She also knew that the time when it is easiest to memorize is in youth.) So many a day Robert sat with his Bible open committing to memory portions from its pages. Probably he often longed to shut the Book and run outside to join his companions in their games, but his mother held him to the task. At twelve years of age he could recite the whole of Psalm 119. That is the longest chapter in the Bible. (Look for yourself and see how many verses there are in it and notice that every verse speaks about the Word of God.)

One day the minister from the Presbyterian Church visited them. He had heard that Robert knew the whole of Psalm 119 by memory. "I would like to have him repeat it in our church," he said.

Next Sunday this twelve-year old boy stood in front of the big congregation and recited the whole of the 119th Psalm. (I wonder if he was nervous? No doubt he was, but he did not make even one mistake in his recitation.)

The congregation went from the church saying, "That boy is not such a dunce after all." Believe it or not, from the time that Robert started to memorize Scripture, he improved in his school work. Soon he was making as much progress as any boy in his class.

Better still, while a boy he gave his heart and life to the Lord Jesus. He wrote out a pledge, which read thus: "Jesus, I have given myself to Thy service. I learn from Thy Word that it is Thy holy pleasure that the Gospel shall be preached to all nations. I desire to go where I am most needed."

Notice that Robert said he learned this from God's Word. In a letter to a friend he told how it was partly the memorizing of Scripture when a boy that influenced him to become a missionary.

In the year 1807 he sailed for China, the very first Protestant missionary. He could hardly have chosen a harder country. Before he could do any work, he must learn the language, and Chinese is the hardest language there is in the world. Someone has said the devil invented the Chinese language so that no missionary could learn it, and thus the Gospel would be kept out of China. Someone else has said that to learn Chinese you must have lungs of steel, a head of oak, eyes of eagles, memories of angels, and the life of Methusalah, who, you will remember, lived longer than any other man. It was this language that Robert, once called the dunce, too stupid to learn, started to study. He not only learned to speak this language like a Chinese person after a time, but he translated the Bible into that language, and wrote an English-Chinese dictionary in six very large volumes.

Today that boy who was known as a dunce is remembered as Robert Morrison, who did a work for China that has probably never been equaled. And it all started with the memorization of Scripture!

What a blessing you may be missing if you have never done any memorization of the Word of God. Why not start now?

(This story is based on incidents from the life of Robert Morrison.)

The Two Roses

"Don't forget Bible Study tonight, Rose."

"I'm sorry, but the gang is going to the movie tonight. I can't back out now, Rose."

"But last week on our Bible Study night you went to the show with them, and you promised then you would keep tonight free."

"It's funny, but everything seems to come on Thursday nights. Better change the Bible Study to some other night, and maybe I'd be there."

"Oh, Rose, don't you care enough about the Bible to keep one night free for it? And I think that crowd you run with are not the kind of friends for a Christian."

"We have fun together," and Rose shrugged her shoulders and was off.

The two girls with the same name were both thirteen years of age, went to the same day school and Sunday school. Both had made their decisions for Christ at the same meeting. There the resemblance ended. Rose Yorke used her influence for Christ in the school. Her testimony was backed by a consistent life. Everyone knew her stand on popular amusements. Rose Martin had been one of a crowd that was rated rather wild, and she made no attempt to separate herself from them after her profession of faith. At that time their Sunday school teacher gave each of the girls a Bible, in which she wrote:

"This Book will keep you from sin.

Sin will keep you from this Book."

Six months later Rose Yorke's Bible was beginning to show signs of wear. Rose Martin's was almost as fresh looking as it was the day that she received it.

Miss Edgar, the Sunday school teacher, noted this and other things with concern. She detained Rose Martin after Sunday school one day. She opened the conversation by saying, "I'm glad you bring your Bible with you to Sunday school, but I wish it did not look so new."

"Why, Miss Edgar, I try to keep it new. I'm so careful of it, and after Sunday school I always put it back in its box."

"And I fear you don't take it out 'til the next Sunday, dear. You will never grow in your Christian life if you don't take time to study your Father's Word."

"There's not much time when one goes to school every day and has to help at home. I'm as busy as can be."

"How many evenings last week did you have time to go to the show, Rose?"

"Maybe three or four. But, Miss Edgar, a girl can't stick at home reading her Bible all the time. She has to have friends and go places."

"God has made us with a desire for companionship, but there are companions that are not for a Christian and places where a Christian should not be seen."

"I know what you mean, Miss Edgar, but my crowd's all right."

"What would your crowd say if you should carry a Bible with you to the movie and say to them, 'I have something good to read to you,' and then draw out your Bible?"

"They'd sure make fun of me."

"Would they make fun of you if you brought along and read to them out of one of those dime novels you keep in your desk? You know they wouldn't; they'd reach for it."

Although Rose laughed, her teacher's serious words touched her conscience, but her love of pleasure and her fear of the ridicule of her worldly friends kept her from changing her course.

Miss Edgar's birthday came on a Saturday that year. Rose Martin planned to give her a rose, with the words, "A rose from Rose." It was with real pleasure she carried a lovely pink rose to the home of her teacher on the Saturday evening. But as she entered the room her pleasure was somewhat spoiled by the sight of a beautiful white rose in a vase on the table.

"A present from Rose Yorke. She said it was 'A rose from Rose,'" explained Miss Edgar.

Slowly Rose unwrapped her gift. "Too bad we both thought of the same thing."

But her teacher assured her there was nothing she wanted more than two roses. "In fact, I believe the Lord meant you girls each to bring me a rose. It makes possible something about which I will tell you, if you come home with me after Sunday school tomorrow."

Rose Martin accompanied her teacher home the next day with some pride. She felt Miss Edgar had shown a special mark of favor to her in choosing her of all the class for her invitation.

In Miss Edgar's sitting room the two roses stood side by side. The white rose was fresh and lovely. But the other one—! Oh, its petals were no longer pink, but dark and spotted. The flower drooped on its stem and looked half dead. When Miss Edgar took away the tissue paper which concealed the receptacles Rose saw that while the white flower was in a vase of water, the pink one had its stem in a bottle half full of ink. Tears came to her eyes.

"Why did you treat my gift so? Didn't you care about it?"

"I care more for the girl who gave me the gift, and I did it with a purpose. Each rose speaks to me, and I hope to you, of what the two givers will be in years to come if they continue as they are doing now. The roses have drawn their nourishment from the liquid in which they stand. It's a parable for Christians. Rose Yorke feeds upon the 'water of the Word.' You feed on the things of the world."

"But surely I don't look like this faded rose!"

"This rose did not look like that all at once either. I placed it in the ink 20 hours ago. In one hour the edges of the petals were tinged with black; in three hours the whole flower was darkened. It continued to get darker and began to wrinkle. With the passing years you will become more and more like the worldly things on which you are feeding, Rose."

Miss Edgar reached for her Bible, and turned to 2 Peter 3:14. "Listen to God's pattern for a Christian's life, 'Be diligent that ye may be found of him in peace without spot, and blameless.' A pure, stainless life is not possible if you neglect the pure water of the Word and live in an atmosphere of worldliness. The color of Christ and the color of sin are totally different. He would have us without spot."

Rose remained quiet a long time, while her teacher silently prayed that the object lesson might speak. Then she said, "I'm not an Indian giver, Miss Edgar, but may I have the rose I gave you? It will be a permanent reminder, in case I forget what you have said."

That is why, on Rose Martin's writing table, there stands a small picture frame. There is no picture in it, only a discolored, spotted rose. And beside it lies a well-worn Bible. Her closest friends, and Rose Yorke is one of them, know why the two are placed together.

The Cow Man's Quarter

We never did know his real name. He was a little man, old, and without a home of his own, as were all the old folks living at the Poor Farm. A group of us from the town two miles away went out to the Farm each week to conduct a Gospel service. We soon grew to recognize this old man, partly because he was always at the service and also because he wore a suit of clothes much, much too big for him. He was such a little man that he looked lost in the clothes which had evidently been given to him by a fairly large man.

Each of the old people at the Farm had a job to do. His was to milk the cows. So, among ourselves, we got to calling him the "cow man."

One day in May there accompanied us to the Poor Farm a young man and his wife who were to leave the next day to do missionary work in South America. After the musical part of the service, these two spoke of their call to a people who go their way (which is Satan's way) in ignorance of the glad news of salvation through Christ.

We always arose at six o'clock in the morning, but that Monday, before we were up, there came a ring at the door. There stood the "cow man." He laid a quarter in the hand of the one who came to the door. "For the McBrides," he said simply. This was the name of the missionary couple.

"Where did you get it?" was the natural question, for we all knew the old people at the Farm were practically penniless.

"Visitor gave it to me. To go to the circus."

"O thank you so much. But come in and see Mr. and Mrs. McBride, and have a rest before you start back."

The "cow man" shook his head, "Have to be back to milk the cows before breakfast."

Back he started over the long route he had just covered, his too-big trousers flapping around his tired old legs.

This happened many years ago in Ohio. The "cow man" must have died long before this. But this story has been told as a memorial to him who gave out of his poverty, sacrificing a pleasure, to speed the Gospel on its way. Probably he never had the chance to see a circus again. I have written down his gift as twenty-five cents. I wonder what value was placed on it by the One Who said of another gift small in money value, but big with sacrifice, (she) "hath cast in more than they all."

A Cup of Cold Water

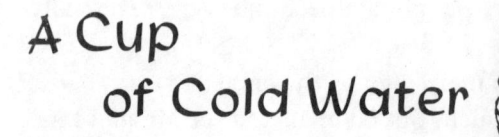

During those hard war days I was in the depot of a large city at one time to bid goodbye to members of my family who were leaving to live elsewhere. I stood with tears in my eyes, taking a last look at beloved faces seen through the train windows. A man came up, touched his cap and said, "A Christian never says goodbye to Christians for the last time." The train pulled out, and I turned to the speaker.

He wore the blue uniform of an employee of the railroad. I asked him, "Are you a Christian?" He replied that he was, adding that he knew I was, for he had heard me speak over the radio.

"I often get an opportunity as I work about the depot to say a word to travelers about the other road they are traveling from time to eternity," he went on. I encouraged him to continue, asking him about his experiences in talking to people. The one that impressed me most was about a time when he did not say a word.

A group of German war prisoners was being conveyed to

a prison camp further west and had to change trains at this depot. Most of them were hardened and sullen looking. But one sat apart from the others—a mere boy. He looked tired, hot and homesick. My new acquaintance said, "I longed to give him the comfort of the Gospel, but we were not permitted to speak with war prisoners; besides, I did not know a word of his language. However, I asked for and received permission to bring him a drink, for the day was very warm. I carried the cup to him filled with cold, clear water. He took it, and his eyes filled with tears; a new light came into his face. I could only hope he understood I was giving him a cup of cold water in Christ's name."

As I left the depot, my heart was warmed by this little story of a man's thought for others.

There are many people in this world to whom a kind deed or word may be like a cup of cold water to a thirsty soul. Even boys and girls can do a thoughtful act, give a bunch of flowers to a sick person, write a cheery note, speak a kind word. To some who may be lonely and discouraged, it will be like the cup of cold water given to that homesick German war prisoner.

Jesus lived for others. He was never too weary or too busy to help those in need. He Himself said, "As my Father hath sent me, even so send I you."

I have just received word from a friend of a summer Bible school in a country district. The theme of the teaching was "Living for Jesus." This was written on the blackboard, so that it might be before the pupils all the time. One night a dance was held in this rural school house. Some of the dancers changed the theme and made it to read thus, "Living for Jes us." The choice is ours; shall our lives be lived for "just us" or for Jesus? If the latter, there will be happiness now and a reward hereafter, for Christ said that even a cup of cold water given in His name shall in no wise lose its reward.

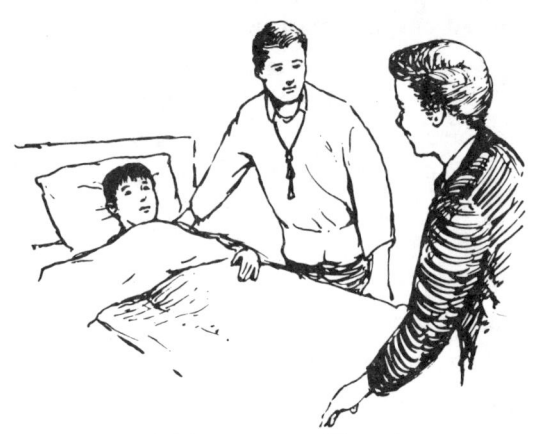

The Hurry-Hurry Song

Pedro had grown to eleven years under the sunny skies of Mexico. He was a bright boy living in a little village in central Mexico up in the mountains.

Pedro was a typical Mexican, for his favorite word was "mañana," which means "after a while" or "tomorrow." No one in Mexico is ever in a hurry, and if you ask them to do something, "Mañana," they say; and the next day, it's "Mañana" again. Pedro was very fond of the word, especially when there was something asked of him which was not to his liking.

One day, while playing with some other boys, he saw a car coming up the narrow mountain road. Soon the car drove into the village and parked. There was a radio playing in it, and soon quite a crowd gathered, for the Mexican is fond of music. Then the man, whose face and hair was much fairer than that of the Mexicans, got out of the car and began to put up a chart. It represented two ways, one broad and one narrow. There were people walking on the two ways.

When Pedro saw that they were Mexican people, the men in their huge sombreros, with serapes over their shoulders, and the women in their rebosos (or shawls), he drew near, for evidently this was not a foreign picture.

The man began to tell them that this picture represented the way God saw all the people in the world walking on one of two roads—a broad road, leading to destruction, and a narrow road, leading to life everlasting. Then he pointed to the large, red cross at the place where the two roads began to divide, and he told them that Christ, the Savior, died on the cross to save them from the destruction at the end of the broad way. He explained that by coming to Him and accepting His salvation, one began walking on the narrow way. When he was finished, he offered a little red book which he called a "Gospel" for one centavo.

Pedro had never had a centavo (about a quarter of a cent) in his life, so he never thought of buying a book, but he lingered around. After the man had taken down the chart and was packing up, he said to the boy, "Will you not cross over to the narrow way by coming to Jesus Christ?"

Pedro showed all his white teeth in a broad smile and said obligingly, "Si, Senor."

"That's good. Suppose you do it now."

But Pedro shook his black head so vigorously that the mass of hair tumbled into his eyes and said, "Mañana, Senor."

The missionary sighed. So often had he heard this answer in Mexico. However, he simply said, "Here's a Gospel for you," handing the boy one of the little red books. "Now you read it, and when I come back I will give you another, a green covered one, with other good words in it, if you have read this one. Will you read it?"

Pedro said he would, and he really meant to do it. But the days passed by so quickly. Every morning he had to go to the stream outside the village to fetch the water for the day's use, and since he never hurried walking there and back and usually went in for a swim with the other boys congregated at the stream, it was noon when he returned. After his midday meal, it was time for the siesta, which every Mexican takes, until about 3 P.M. In the afternoon sugar cane had to be cut, and sometimes wood hauled from the forest, and, of course, a little play, and so the days passed by and the little book was unread.

About a month later the missionary returned, and Pedro was there to welcome him.

"Have you read the little book?" asked the man, whose name, he told the boy, was Mr. Gordon.

"Not yet."

"O, I'm sorry. When will you read it?"

And Pedro replied promptly, "Mañana."

When the morrow came Pedro had other things to think of, for he was very sick—doubled up with pain. All day long he suffered, and he got worse in spite of all his father and mother tried to do for him.

The following day he was no better. A neighbor came in and spoke to the father. "There is a place of healing in Cuernavaca run by the evangelicals. One of them was preaching here yesterday. You had better take your boy there. He looks very sick."

And the father said, "We will go to Cuernavaca, for we can do nothing more for the boy."

So Pedro was placed on the back of a burro (a donkey)

and was made as comfortable as possible by his mother. But oh, that journey! Nobody hurries in Mexico, but the burro hurries least of all. All day long they jogged up and down the mountain trail covering the ten miles to Cuernavaca. How Pedro suffered! It was a very tired and sick boy who was at last lifted off the burro and put to bed in the hospital.

The doctor came to look at him. Along with him came another man, and lo, it was Pedro's friend who preached in the village. He explained that the doctor had only newly come to this land and knew little Spanish, though he did know all about sickness, so Mr. Gordon would interpret for him.

A few questions were asked and answered, and then the doctor and Mr. Gordon talked together in English.

"Is my boy very sick?" asked the father.

"Yes," replied Mr. Gordon in Spanish, "he is a very sick lad."

"Can you do anything for him?"

"We think we can."

"When?" asked Pedro, who had been listening.

Mr. Gordon started to speak, then checked himself, and after a pause, replied, "Mañana."

"O Senor Gordon," wailed Pedro, "I cannot, I cannot wait. The pain is so great I can't stand another night of it!"

"Is it not dangerous to wait?" asked Pedro's father.

"It is always dangerous to wait when it is a matter of life and death," said Mr. Gordon, with emphasis, looking at Pedro, "We will operate NOW."

Several weeks later Pedro lay in the white hospital bed thinking over what had happened. He remembered the long, painful journey, and he thought of the despair in his heart when he heard Senor Gordon say they would relieve him "Mañana." He remembered nothing of the operation, because the doctor had given him something to put him to sleep, but he did remember the visit of Senor Gordon a few days later, when he sat beside Pedro's bed and told him that he had purposely said "Mañana" about the operation to bring home to Pedro the danger of delay in eternal matters.

"The operation only affected your body, although the delay would have meant death; but delay in accepting Christ is more dangerous, for your eternal destiny will be affected, Pedro." He added a little more explanation about the two ways, and the entrance on the narrow way through the cross of Christ.

Pedro thought of all this now, and just then he heard sweet voices in the patio of the hospital. It was the children of the Evangelical Sunday School singing this Sunday afternoon for the patients. And the song they sang was:

"Come to the Savior, make no delay,
 Here in His Word He has shown us the way,
 Here in our midst He is standing today,
 Tenderly saying, 'Come.'"

When they stopped singing, Pedro put his little brown hands together and said, "Jesus Christ, I come NOW."

The next time Mr. Gordon visited him, he told him all about it, and, of course, the missionary rejoiced.

Then Pedro said, "O Senor, when can I go home? Soon?"

"Pedro, you have never been in a hurry before! Why are you so anxious to get home?"

"O Senor, I want to tell them about Jesus Christ and to sing for them the 'hurry-hurry song.'"

"The 'hurry-hurry song'?"

"Why, yes, you know, 'Come to the Savior, make no delay.' That means hurry, hurry, doesn't it? O tell me, when can I go?"

And the missionary smiled at the eager face and replied, "Mañana."

"O now, Senor, you are just joking me and giving me back my own word."

"No, really Pedro, the doctor says you may go tomorrow. And we will be praying for you that your testimony and the 'hurry-hurry song' may bring some to see the danger of delay in accepting Jesus Christ."